NAG CLUB

Harold
H
Petra
Anna
Archie

Charlotte

Other young books by Anne Fine:

Care of Henry

How to Cross the Road and Not Turn into a Pizza

The Haunting of Pip Parker

The Jamie and Angus Stories

Jamie and Angus Together

Jamie and Angus Forever

Under a Silver Moon

ANNE FINE

NAG CLUB

illustrated by Arthur Robins

WALKER
BOOKS

For Ione, when young...
A.F.

First published 2004 by Walker Books Ltd
87 Vauxhall Walk, London SE11 5HJ

This edition published 2012

4 6 8 10 9 7 5 3

This book has been typeset in Garamond

Printed in China

British Library Cataloguing in Publication Data:
a catalogue record for this book is available from the British Library

ISBN 978-1-4063-4182-9

www.walker.co.uk

Contents

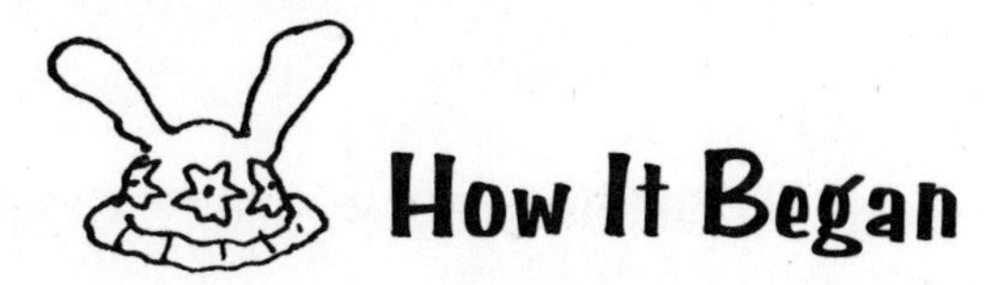

How It Began

It began because everyone wanted a boggle hat. They were brilliant. They came in all different sorts.

Some with long floppy ears like rabbits.

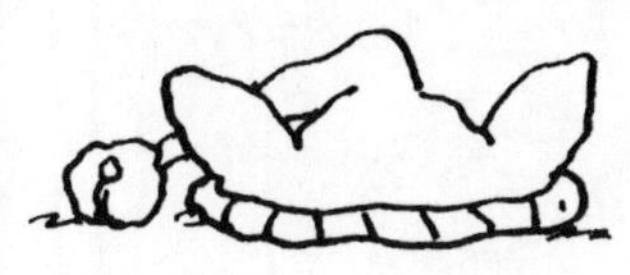

Some with pert little ears like elves.

Some were sweet.

Some looked scary.

And one or two were downright horrible.

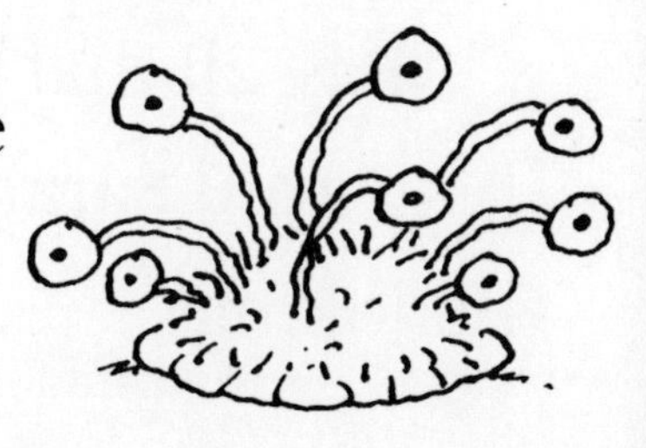

The only trouble was, they cost the earth.

"Pay all that for a stupid little hat?" said Sarah's dad. "You must be joking!"

"Forget it, Jack!" his mum told him. "You need new shoes, and you're already growing out of your jacket. I'm not wasting money on a silly hat that won't even keep your ears warm."

And all the other parents said the same. Only Lola had a boggle hat. The rest were still in the window of the shop on the corner.

Petra peered through the glass and sighed. "I want one *sooooo* much." She pointed to the one with furry black cat ears. "That one!"

She turned to Lola. "How did you get your mum and dad to buy you yours?"

"Easy," said Lola. "I whined. I always whine when I really, really want something. In fact, I've had to whine quite hard for everything I've ever wanted."

"I might try that," said Petra.

"So will I," said Jack.

"Let's all try," said Charlotte, who liked doing things in gangs.

"Whining won't work for everyone," said Lola. "You have to pick the right nag for your family."

Everyone stared.

Lola stared back. "Don't you people know *anything* about getting what you want? Do I have to start a club and give you all *lessons*?"

"Yes, please!" yelled everyone. "Yes, Lola! Start a club and give us lessons."

Lesson One: The "Oh, Please, Please, *Please!*" Nag

"Right," Lola said. "We'll start with the basic 'oh, please, please, *please*!' nag."

Everyone had a go.

"More desperate," Lola told them. "More as if you've been crawling for days over hot desert sands, and suddenly someone is standing right in front of you with a glass of cool sparkling water."

Everyone tried again.

"That's much, much better," said Lola.

Archie stepped into the ring. He made his eyes go round. He spread his hands out like a little match-seller with bare feet begging for money in a snowstorm to feed his starving baby. He made his voice go trembly.

he whimpered.

"If you don't let me have a boggle hat, I think I'm going to *die*. I'm not sure I can *live* without a boggle hat. In fact, I'm sure I can't. I'm sure I'll never, ever, ever be happy again until I have one of those boggle hats in the shop on the corner. Oh, please! Oh, please! Oh, pretty, pretty please! Please let me have a boggle hat like Lola's. *Pleeeeease!*"

Everyone clapped.

"That's very good," said Lola. "Do it again, and everyone listen carefully."

Archie did it again.

"Right," Lola said. "Everyone go home tonight and do your best. I'll see you all in the morning."

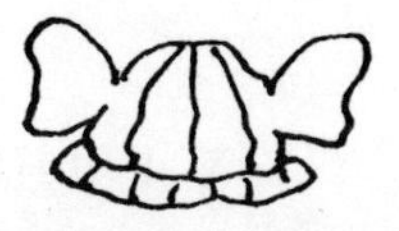

Lesson Two: The Sugar-Coated Nag

Next morning, Archie and Sarah had boggle hats, but nobody else did.

"My mother sent me up to bed," said Harold. "She said she was sick to death of hearing me whingeing."

"So did my mother," said Anna. "*And* she stopped my pocket money for a week."

Lola didn't seem bothered. "You'll just have to try another way. We'll do the sugar-coated nag next. That often works on people who can't stand pleaders."

Archie and Sarah hung round the edge of the circle. Archie was in his new boggle hat with the spotty ears, and Sarah was wearing the one with the fur wisps.

"I'm staying to listen," Archie explained to Sarah, "in case I ever really want something else."

"Makes sense," said Sarah. And she stayed as well.

Lola stepped into the circle. She turned to Anna and put on a really soppy smile.

"Mumm-*eee*," she warbled. "I love you so, *sooooo* much. I think you're the best mummy in the whole wide world. I think you're wonderful. You're clever, and kind, and you can do anything. *Anything*."

She waited a
few moments.

Everyone waited with her.

"And can I have one of those lovely boggle hats down at the corner shop?" she added.

Anna shook her head. "It's very *good*," she admitted. "But I'm not sure it's going to work because I can't do the 'Mumm-*eee*' bit. You see, I live with my dad and Maria."

"Dads are easier," Lola assured her. "You can get round a dad in no time at all."

"All right. I'll try it," said A

She stepped into the circle.

"Dadd-*eee*!" she said to the air around her. "You know that I love you, don't you? You know that I love you more than anything in the whole wide world—"

"That's good!" said Lola. "That 'whole wide world' bit always helps. Keep going."

Anna kept going.

"Dadd-*eee*, you know that I love you more than everything on the planet. I love you more than television and apricot ice cream and caramel bars and roller skating and even the new scary ride at Sandover Park, and I love you more than my new silver jacket, and *everything*!"

She waited a moment.

"Well, can I have a boggle hat?" she finished, and took a bow while the rest of them clapped.

"Good!" Lola told her. "Let's see if it works!"

Lesson Three: The Getting a Bit Nasty Nag

It didn't work. Anna came back to school next morning without a boggle hat. But Petra had one.

"It worked on *my* dad," she announced. "No problem. He just went pink with pleasure, then spun Mum some yarn about needing some longer Rawlplugs, and we went shopping. I didn't even have to finish my homework first."

"You must be very cruel to him usually," suggested Charlotte.

Petra gave this some thought.

"Yes," she said, blushing. "Maybe I am, a bit. I think that, in future, I might try to be nicer."

Lola asked Jack, "What happened to you?"

Jack shrugged. "I tried it on my mum," he confessed. "But she only said, 'Don't try to soft-soap me!' and added that, if I loved her all that much, I could polish the sideboard and dining table for her."

"And did you?" Harold asked.

"Yes. Yes, I did."

"And did she say that, as a reward, she'd buy you a boggle hat tomorrow?" persisted Harold.

"No," Jack said. "She only said that it was nice to see me pulling my weight around the house for a change. Then she slid off next door to have a quick drink with her friend Nesta."

"You're going to have to get tough," warned Lola. "I know you're still a bit new to this, but it seems to me that you may have to move on to the getting a bit nasty nag."

Jack gave Lola a smart military salute. "Ready to go, ma'am! Just show me."

"It's a useful one," Lola said. "So I'll show everyone."

She turned to face them. "After me."

Everyone stood up straight and took deep breaths.

"You *have* to buy me that boggle hat!" wailed Lola. "It isn't *fair*! You *never* buy me anything I want. You're really *mean* to me! I want a boggle hat!"

"I'm not going home and saying that," said Harold. "I'd end up being sent to bed."

He made a face. "Or *worse*."

"So would I," Anna said. "I'm not trying that either."

"Nor me," said Charlotte.

"I might," said Jack. "But only on my great-granny. I go to her on Wednesdays, and she puts up with a lot."

“Then why not try one of the earlier nags on her?” Lola suggested. “The sugar-coated nag. Or even the basic ‘oh, please, please, *please*!’ one?”

“I might,” said Jack. “That would be nicer, wouldn’t it?”

“And it would probably work a whole lot faster,” Lola assured him. “Part of the skill of nagging is matching the method to the victim.”

"Right," said Jack. "I'll try the first nag we learned on Great-Granny."

"What about us?" complained Charlotte. "What about me and Harold and Anna? What are we going to do to get our boggle hats? What's left for us?"

"I'll tell you tomorrow," said Lola. "But I'm going home now."

And she and Archie went off in their boggle hats after Sarah and Petra.

Lesson Four: The Pity Poor Me Nag

Next morning, Jack showed up in his new boggle hat.

"Piece of cake!" he explained. "I'd only just begun and I got a kiss and a boggle hat from Great-Granny 'just for saying the magic word without being reminded'."

"What *was* the magic word?" everyone asked, curious.

"It was 'please'," Jack confessed. "I must try it more often."

The rest looked rather jealous, so Lola stepped in to distract them with a lesson.

"This next one's a good nag," said Lola. "But it does take time. If you try rushing it, everyone gets irritated. It's important to start slowly, so they don't lose patience."

"How do you start?" asked Anna.

"Well," Lola said. "First you go quiet and mope about a bit. Then, when they ask what's wrong, you just say 'Nothing' over and over." She wagged a warning finger round the circle. "You mustn't tell them too soon, or they catch on."

"Right," Charlotte said, recapping the main point. "Go all quiet."

"What then?" asked Harold.

"Then," said Lola, "you vanish somewhere in the house. Pretend you don't hear when they call. And let them find you sitting all alone, hunched over on a carpet in some cold room miles away from everyone, looking all sad, and drawing patterns on the floor with your fingertips."

"Why drawing patterns with your fingertips?" asked Harold.

"I don't know," Lola said. "All I know is, it works."

"What then?"

"Then, next time they ask you what's wrong, say what you said before – 'Nothing' – but, this time, burst into tears."

Everyone stared.

"Can you do that?" Charlotte asked Lola. "Just burst into tears?"

"I've done a lot of practising," Lola admitted.

"I'm sure I couldn't do it," Harold said.

"Oh, you'll soon learn," said Lola airily. "But the tears don't matter too much anyway. Just make sure you do the sad sniffle. The only really important thing is getting the words right."

"What words?"

"There are quite a few of them," Lola warned them. "And you do have to get them right. So shall we practise?"

Everyone stood in line to practise.

"After me!" Lola said.

She took a very deep breath.

"I just feel sad," she said.

Everyone else took a deep breath and copied her.

"I just feel sad," they chorused after her.

Everyone *else* has a boggle hat.
Everyone *else* has a boggle hat.
And I heard someone whispering that our family was too *poor* to buy me a boggle hat.

And I heard someone whispering that our family was too *poor* to buy me a boggle hat.
I'll be all right. I don't mind *really*. I'm just a little *sad*.
I'll be all right. I don't mind *really*. I'm just a little *sad*.

Harold didn't join in the last line. He was very polite. He waited till the rest had finished practising, and then he said, "I'm not trying that nag, Lola."

"Why not?" Lola asked.

"Because it's mean," said Harold. "It doesn't give them a fair chance.

And it will make them feel terrible."

Anna and Charlotte agreed.

"I'd rather not have a boggle hat at all," Anna admitted. "If I got one this way, I wouldn't ever want to wear it. It would be spoiled for me. Can we miss this nag out?"

"Sure," Lola said cheerfully. "But if you don't want to do that nag, you probably won't want to do the last three, either."

"Why? Which are they?"

"Tell you in lesson five," said Lola. "And that's tomorrow."

So everyone went home – some in their boggle hats and some without.

Lesson Five: The Rude Nag, the Huffy Nag and the Blazing Tantrum

Everyone enjoyed the lesson, especially trying the blazing tantrum.

Charlotte lay on the floor and kicked her heels and screamed and yelled until all of the infants came over to watch her.

Anna preferred the huffy nag.

"I suppose you don't *care*," she told everyone. "I suppose you think what I want doesn't *matter*. I suppose you think just because I'm the youngest in the family, you don't have to listen to anything *I* say. You can treat me like *rubbish*!"

"That's very good," Lola told her.

She turned to Harold. "That only leaves the rude nag. Can you do that?"

"I could *try*," said Harold shyly.

He stepped into the middle of the circle and put his hands on his hips.

You're a pig! I *hate* you! You're mean and ugly and *horrible.* I hope you spill soup down your best clothes and get spots on your nose. I hope your bathwater runs stone cold for a week, you catch worms off the cat, and everyone forgets your birthday on Saturday.

"Brilliant!" said Charlotte. "That is very rude. I wouldn't dare say that."

"Neither would I," admitted Harold. "That's why I've spent the whole week cleaning cars for money."

He dug in his pocket …

…and drew out a brand new boggle hat.

"And bought this!"

It was the one with a space creature's antennae where the ears should be.

Charlotte and Anna looked at one another.

"Neat idea," said Anna.

"Better than rolling on the ground in a tantrum," said Charlotte.

They turned to Lola. "Would you mind?" said Charlotte. "Would you be very hurt if we just *earned* the money instead?"

Lola shrugged. "Whatever works. Anything, so long as everyone in Nag Club ends up with a boggle hat."

And in the end, of course,
everyone did.

Harold
Petra
Anna
Archie

Jack
Charlotte
Sarah
Lola

Anne Fine is a distinguished writer for both adults and children. She has won numerous awards for her children's books, including the Carnegie Medal twice, the Whitbread Children's Book of the Year Award twice, the Smarties Book Prize and the Guardian Children's Fiction Prize. In 2001, Anne became Children's Laureate and in 2003, she was awarded an OBE and fellowship of the Royal Society of Literature. Her other titles for Walker Books include *Care of Henry*; *How to Cross the Road and Not Turn into a Pizza*; *The Haunting of Pip Parker*; the Jamie and Angus series; and *Under a Silver Moon*. Anne has two grown-up daughters and lives in County Durham.

You can find out more about Anne Fine and her books by visiting her website at:

www.annefine.co.uk